D0065898

My Brother, Ant

A Viking Easy-to-Read

by Betsy Byars
illustrations by Marc Simont

VIKING

Somerset County Library
Bridgewater, NJ   08807

To Benjamin
—B. B.

To Sam and his brother, Michael
—M. S.

VIKING
Published by the Penguin Group
Penguin Books USA Inc., 375 Hudson Street, New York, New York 10014, U.S.A.
Penguin Books Ltd, 27 Wrights Lane, London W8 5TZ, England
Penguin Books Australia Ltd, Ringwood, Victoria, Australia
Penguin Books Canada Ltd, 10 Alcorn Avenue, Toronto, Ontario, Canada M4V 3B2
Penguin Books (N.Z.) Ltd, 182–190 Wairau Road, Auckland 10, New Zealand

Penguin Books Ltd, Registered Offices: Harmondsworth, Middlesex, England

First published in 1996 by Viking,
a division of Penguin Books USA Inc.

1   3   5   7   9   10   8   6   4   2

Text copyright © Betsy Byars, 1996
Illustrations copyright © Marc Simont, 1996
All rights reserved

LIBRARY OF CONGRESS CATALOGING-IN-PUBLICATION DATA
Byars, Betsy Comer.
My brother, Ant / by Betsy Byars;
illustrated by Marc Simont.   p.   cm.—(Viking easy-to-read)
Summary: In four separate stories, Ant's older brother gets rid of the monster under Ant's
bed, forgives Ant for drawing on his homework, tries to read a story, and helps Ant write a
letter to Santa.
ISBN 0-670-86664-4
[1. Brothers—Fiction.] I. Simont, Marc, ill. II. Title. III. Series.
PZ7.B9836My 1996 [E]—dc20   95-23725 CIP AC

Printed in Singapore   Set in New Century Schoolbook

Viking® and Easy-to-Read® are registered trademarks of Penguin Books USA Inc.

Without limiting the rights under copyright reserved above, no part of this
publication may be reproduced, stored in or introduced into a retrieval system,
or transmitted, in any form or by any means (electronic, mechanical,
photocopying, recording or otherwise), without the prior written permission
of both the copyright owner and the above publisher of this book.

Reading level 1.7

THE MONSTER
UNDER ANT'S BED

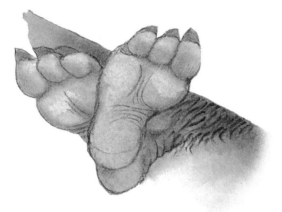

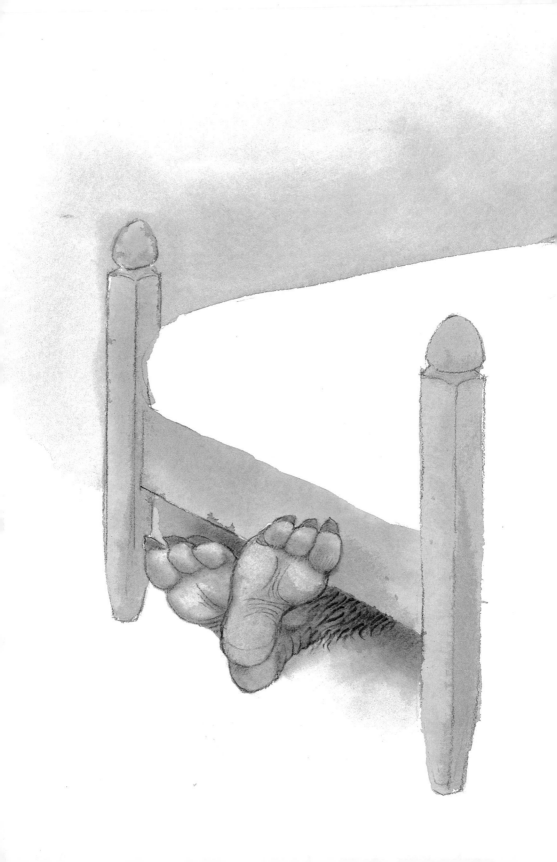

"Ant is crying, Dad.

I can't get to sleep."

I went into the living room

and told this to my dad.

"What's wrong with Anthony?"

my dad asked.

"He says there is a monster

under his bed," I said.

My dad said, "Tell Anthony

there is no monster

under his bed."

"You tell him, Dad.

He won't believe me," I said.

"Anthony!" my dad called.

"This is your dad!

There is no monster

under your bed.

Now go to sleep."

I went back into the bedroom.

I said to the Ant,

"Did you hear what Dad said?"

Ant said, "How does he know?

He didn't look."

I said, "Do you want me to look?"

"You can look," Ant said,

"but you won't see the monster.

He hides from big people."

I pointed to myself.

"This is a big person?

THIS is a big person?

Get real."

I bent down

and looked under the bed.

"All right, Monster," I said.

"Do you see him?" Ant said.

I said, "This is between me

and the monster.

You stay out of this.

"All right, Monster.

Listen up.

Ant does not want you

under his bed.

I do not want you

under his bed.

Get lost."

Then a voice said,

"BOO-HOO-HOO.

WHAT'S A MONSTER TO DO?"

"Find another bed," I said.

"WHERE?" it said.

"That is your problem."

"OH, ALL RIGHT.

BOO-HOO-HOO.

I'M GOING. BYE."

I got up.

"Well, he's gone now," I said.

Ant said, "Was that really the monster?

It sounded like you."

"Me?"

"Yes, you."

"Well, what does it matter?" I said.

"He's gone, isn't he?"

"Yes," said Ant.

"So, can you go to sleep now?"

"Yes."

"Good night, Ant."

ANT AND THE SPIDER

"Mom, Ant drew a spider
on my homework."
Ant came into the kitchen.
"I did not," he said.
"He did too. Look.
I had done all my spelling words.
They were perfect.

"I went out to play,

and I came back and found *that*.

A spider on my homework.

Ant drew a spider

on my homework!"

Ant said, "I did not."

My mother looked at me,

and she looked at the Ant.

She said, "Anthony, tell the truth.

Did you draw a spider

on your brother's homework?"

Ant said, "No, I did not."

"He did too. Look."

I held out the paper.

My mother looked at the black lines.

She looked at the Ant.

She said, "Anthony does not lie.

If he says he did not draw a spider

on your homework,

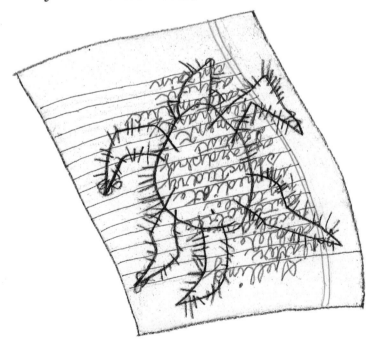

then he did not draw a spider

on your homework."

I stomped out of the room.

Ant came, too.

I said, "I am not talking to you.

You drew that spider.

And you know it."

"I did not."

"Liar!"

"No, give me the paper,

and I'll show you."

Ant took my homework paper.

He turned it around.

He said, "See? It is a dog.

You were looking at it upside down.

It is not a spider.

It is a dog lying on his back."

"A what?"

"A dog on his back.

Here are his four legs.

A spider has more legs than that.

Here is his tail.

A spider has no tail.

So I did not draw a spider

on your homework."

I looked at the paper.

I got ready to yell,

"Mom, Ant drew an upside-down dog

on my homework!"

Ant stopped me.

He said, "You should have known

it was not a spider.

You are the smartest brother

in the world.

Look at all these words you wrote."

I took my pencil.

On the bottom of the page,

I wrote a note to my teacher:

The words are by me.

The upside-down dog is by the Ant.

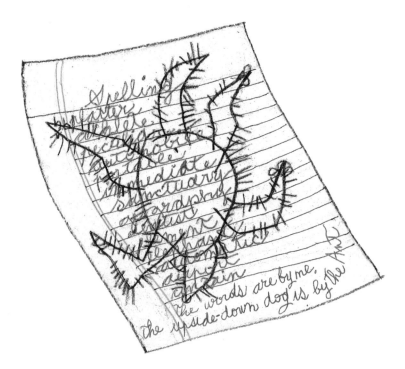

ANT AND THE
THREE LITTLE FIGS

Ant said, "Read me a story."

I like to read.

I said, "Okay."

Ant sat down by me.

I opened the book and began to read.

"Once upon a time

there were three little figs."

Ant sat up.

He said, "No! That is not right.

It's pigs. Three little PIGS.

Say PIGS."

I am easy to get along with.

I said, "Pigs."

The Ant leaned back.

He said, "Now read the story."

I read: "Once upon a time

there were three little bananas."

Ant said, "No! Don't do that!

Read the story right.

It's pigs.

Look at the picture.

There's a pig.

There's a pig.

There's a pig.

Three pigs!"

"Oh, all right. Pigs.

Once upon a time

there were three little—"

"Pigs," Ant said quickly.

"Who is reading this—

you or me?" I asked.

"You are," Ant said,

"but you have to say pigs."

"And you have to let me read.

Once upon a time

there were three little—"

I stopped and waited.

The Ant waited, too.

Finally he said,

"This is your last chance.

If you don't say pigs, I'm leaving."

I said, "Oh, all right.

Once upon a time

there were three little pigs. . . ."

Ant got down from the chair.

I said, "Where are you going, Ant?

I read it right. I said pigs."

Ant said, "I am going outside."

"Why, Ant?"

"I don't like the rest of the story.

It has a big bad wolf in it."

I said, "I could change that, Ant.

I could make him a big bad lemon.

Or how about a big bad watermelon?"

"No," said Ant,

"I would know it was a wolf."

Ant went to the door and opened it.

He looked back at me.

He said, "But thank you

for reading to me."

"You are welcome, Ant,"

I said, "anytime."

LOVE, ANT

"Will you write a letter for me?"

Ant asked.

I like to write letters.

I said, "Okay."

I got some paper and a pencil.

Ant said, "Are you ready?"

I nodded.

Ant said, "The letter starts:

Dear Santa."

I said, "Santa! Santa? It is July.

Nobody writes to Santa in July!"

Ant said, "I do."

I said, "You don't get it, Ant.

You wait till December.

Then you write to Santa.

You say, 'Give me this.'

You say, 'Give me that.'

If you write in July,

he won't remember."

"Just write the words," Ant said.

"All right," I said.

"*Dear Santa—*"

I wrote that.

"*Thank you for last Christmas.*

I still like my presents."

I wrote that.

"Is that it, Ant?" I asked.

"Except for the end."

"How do you want to end it?" I said.

Ant said, "The usual way: *Love, Ant.*"

"Good ending," I said.

"Thank you," said the Ant.